HATE
TO
LOVE

VALERIE PEPPER

For all the reality television shows about love, and those who watch them

Chapter 1

Charlotte

"ABSOLUTELY NOT."

"Look at that—something we finally agree on."

"Oh, go to hell, Levi."

He smirks, the curve of his full lips just as distracting as they've always been. "That would mean living with you, and apparently we're doing that for the next twenty-four hours. It seems, my dear, I'm very much already there."

I hate him. Hate him so much.

And I can't believe Levi Hall, of all people, is ruining this for me. My one chance at finding love. It sounds dramatic, I know, but between working eighty-hour weeks and caring for my father, there is absolutely no time for dating. Not that there are any guys out there worth my time. So this experiment was supposed to be my silver bullet. Twenty-four hours with a stranger in a house.

Only the stranger is very much not one.

In fact, he may well be my greatest enemy.

Reaching deep, I take a deep breath and center myself, then turn my best attempt at doe eyes on the show's producers. "See, we already know each other."

"You don't think they've figured that out?" Levi interrupts, the very timbre of his voice sending fury streaking through my veins.

"Wasn't talking to you, *jerk*." I whip my head back to Rhiva and Ulman, dropping all pretense and going for the kill. "How is there nothing in the rules that says participants can't know each other first?"

They glance at each other, then me. Rhiva shrugs. "There just isn't."

Ulman waves the contracts we signed in my face. "These are iron clad."

"For…reasons," Rhiva adds.

Ulman glares at Rhiva. "Obviously. Ones we don't need to talk about. And it means you'll be staying in the house together, for twenty-four hours, even if you don't like each other."

Levi gestures at them and raises a thick eyebrow. "I gotta say, Counselor, they're not wrong." If there was an award for the most holier than thou attitude given, Levi Hall would win it. Hands down.

I roll my eyes. "Don't talk down to me, *Counselor*. I'm the one who wins the cases, remember?"

His cheeks tinge pink so subtly that if I hadn't known him for a decade, I would have missed it.

It's beyond gratifying.

"Nevertheless," he moves on, ignoring my flawless jab, "given the new information you've presented, we'd like twenty-four hours to review the contracts in more detail."

"That's not possible," Ulman states.

"Anything is possible," Levi replies smoothly, his manner suggesting he rarely hears the word *no*.

Except when I wipe the floor with him in the courtroom.

His eyes flick to me for the briefest of seconds as he holds his hand out for the contract we both signed.

Which we did willingly, I might add. To my abject and continuing horror.

The participant, Charlotte Kelly, agrees to remain on the premises with the other participant for twenty-four hours. During this time, both participants agree to be filmed. Participants may not leave the premises. Premises include the following…

It's a contract a first-year law student could get through: simple, but effective.

One that I thought—erroneously, I now see—might have the power to change my life. To finally open the door to me living again. *Really* living. Not just going through the motions that I promised my mother before she died.

"For the final time, Mr. Hall, what's done is done." Rhiva folds their arms and squares their shoulders.

Levi glares at the two of them, not stepping down from the fight in the least. He can look all he wants; I reviewed that thing to within an inch of its life before I signed it, and it's locked down tight. I had to fight tooth and nail to get the emergency clause written in that guarantees they'll alert me if something goes wrong with my father or sister, so I'm well-versed in the contract's language.

His desire to review it again is almost admirable. Almost. One thing the man clearly hasn't mastered is the art of admitting defeat.

Must be nice. Wonder if that's a man thing, or just a Levi thing?

Regardless, I'm over it. With a look at Rhiva and Ulman, and a dismissive snort at the man my clients have repeatedly called Satan himself, I deliver my first closing statement of the day. "Get over yourself, Levi. We're stuck together."

Grabbing my overnight bag, I swivel and make my way across the asphalt into the house, my hips sashaying for all they're worth.

The show starts now.

CHAPTER 2

LEVI

FUCK. ME. TWENTY-four hours with this woman is going to kill me.

Actually, who knows? Maybe I'm already dead, and this is my own personal hell. It would be fitting.

Forcing myself to face the producers in front of me and not watch the mesmerizing sway of Charlotte Kelly's generous hips as she saunters into the house of doom, I scrub a hand over my face and bite back a curse. "I'm not going to ask again. Hand it over." I raise to my full height and extend a hand. I've used my size to my advantage my entire life, and I am not about to stop using it now.

Ulman raises an eyebrow at my display, not intimidated in the least, but hands it to me nonetheless. "Iron clad," he repeats.

With a grunt, I grab the contract, turn my back on him, and scan it once more. I know it's tightly woven, and unless a miracle presents itself right this very moment, there's nothing in here that I've missed. But that doesn't mean I won't use the few minutes to gather myself.

Charlotte Kelly.

Charlotte Kelly.

Of all the people, in all the world, *this* is the woman that shows up in front of me. A force of nature with hazel eyes that have always seemed to find my every weakness and exploit it to her advantage. The woman I beat by the skin of my teeth to graduate top of our law school class a decade ago. The woman who got the same job offers as me from the top firms in the country. The woman who, bafflingly, took none of them and instead seemed to disappear off the face of the planet. The woman who then reappeared across from me in court five years later, the time apart having made her even more devastating, and proceeded to fucking *win the case.*

And I never lose.

Ever.

Which is bad enough. But then there's this, the most insane, cruel twist of fate imaginable, where *she's* the one paired with *me* for the future entertainment of millions. Because in one momentary blip of insanity, I applied to this show in some ridiculous effort to, what, find true love? As if something like that is even possible these days.

Mentally adding the moment of weakness that led to me participating in this show to my towering pile of regrets, I whirl around and shove the contract back at Ulman. "No cameras in the bedrooms. Section five, paragraph one."

"Bedroom," Rhiva corrects. "One. Bedroom."

My jaw ticks. Of course. The whole point of the show is to force participants together in every moment possible, to see if they are willing to date beyond the twenty-four hours they're stuck together. Assuming they don't kill each other first. And right now, there's a distinct possibility that Charlotte will murder me in my sleep through the sheer force of her hatred alone. Not that I'd blame her. My clients are fucking monsters. "Bedroom. No camera."

Ulman nods, a smile slithering across his reptilian face.

"Are we done here? The clock is ticking," Rhiva says, a pointed lift of their eyebrow.

I check my wristwatch. It's not even nine a.m. and I'm already exhausted. But I've committed to this charade, and if nothing else, twenty-four hours of blissful time away from my clients is worth something. Readjusting my bag across my body and stepping around them, I send the command over my shoulder. "Start rolling. Let's get this over with."

CHAPTER 3

CHARLOTTE

I'VE DECIDED THIS is like that whole "airport time" thing I've seen on social media, where the *actual* time ceases to exist and rules about what's socially acceptable cease to exist. And sure, nine a.m. is a little early to drink, but I need something to calm my nerves, and meditation is not an option. Naturally, the producers have ensured that all manner of alcohol is in the house, so I'm a third of the way through a healthy pour of Pinot Grigio by the time Levi appears.

His sharp, assessing gaze goes immediately to the cameras in the corners of the ceiling, then darts to other places a camera might be: the ficus plant, the lamp, the bookshelf with absolutely no books. He clenches a strong hand around the duffel strap crossing his massive chest, and that's when I stop looking.

Levi Hall has been a pain in my ass since the second day of law school. He not only talked over me in Intro to Litigation, he also made me feel like shit in the process.

I've never forgotten it, and I've sure as hell never let another man talk over me *or* make me feel less than in the years since. Beating him soundly in the courtroom has been, without question, some of the most satisfying moments of my life.

He stalks out of the room without so much as looking my way. I can't help the way my eyes land on his backside as he departs. He may be a pain in my ass, but his own ass happens to be quite delightful to behold.

Do you have any idea how difficult it is to show off an ass in business slacks? Those things don't make anyone look good. And yet of course Levi Hall manages to do it effortlessly. Life itself seems to just roll over and present its belly to him, happy to let him be the alpha. The one thing he *can't* do so effortlessly, though? Win.

Not against me, anyway.

Doesn't make me detest him any less.

"There's only one bed." He returns to the living room, making the statement as though it's breaking news.

I meet his dark blue eyes. "Of course there's only one bed. It's a dating show."

"No cameras, though."

For the briefest of moments, his tone isn't haughty. It's calm, resolute. And in those seconds, I feel protected. Something I've not felt in literal decades. Then I remember that Levi is a top tier asshole and is only out for himself and his piece of shit clients, and there's no way he's being sincere. I toss him a grin. "You got a complex about something, Levi?"

His expression darkens, sending a thrill through me. "I'll play you for it."

I blink. "Excuse me?"

He gestures towards the bookcase and the stack of games in it. "Uno. Winner takes the bed."

Smirking and shaking my head, I say, "You'll be perfectly comfortable on the couch, Levi." He won't be—the couch looks pretty but is shorter than he is tall and incredibly uncomfortable—but I'm not about to let facts get in the way of a good story. Not right now. Not when the stakes are this high.

"That's not how this is going to work."

I cross my arms and pop a hip out. "Figures you wouldn't do the gentlemanly thing."

"Figures *you'd* be like that," he scoffs.

I bristle. "Like what?"

He steps towards me, close enough for me to catch his masculine scent. It's the closest we've been since we sat next to each other in third year ethics. Not by choice, for what it's worth. He annoyed and distracted me then, and he's absolutely doing the same thing now. The problem is that this time, there's nothing to win. Only everything to lose.

"You're smart, Charlotte. *Too* smart, if there is such a thing. I'm sure you can figure out what I mean."

The way my breath hitches is a manifestation of my hatred for him. It has nothing to do with the heat coming off him. Or the way his full lips rise infinitesimally. "Fuck you," I bite out.

His smile is feral. "In your dreams, sweetheart."

CHAPTER 4

LEVI

NEVER IN MY life have I had more fun pissing someone off. Watching Charlotte Kelly's substantial breasts heave as she takes breath after breath, clearly trying to convince herself not to pummel me in front of the cameras that are positioned to get our every angle, is the most fun I've had in ages. Maybe this won't be so bad after all.

"So." I clap my hands together and stride to the bookshelf, then brandish the Uno deck. "Are you in?"

She snaps out of the haze of hatred she's wrapped herself in, her hazel eyes flashing as she lifts her chin. "Prepare to lose. Like you always do."

It's a cheap shot, and she knows it. Still, I can't argue with her. The woman has prevailed in all three cases we've had against each other. And every time, I thought I had it in the bag. Every time, I thought I'd considered every angle. And every damn time, she flattened me. She pisses me off like no one else, but I respect the hell out of her. And honestly? My clients *should* have lost every one of those cases. They deserved the financial hit they took, and each night after those losses, I sent a prayer of thanks to her as I drank myself stupid.

Not that I would ever let her know that.

I unbox the cards and begin shuffling as I stand. "That remains to be seen."

She smirks, then gestures to the tiny kitchen table. "After you."

"Classic rules." It's not a question.

"Obviously. They're the *only* rules."

"I concur." We take our seats across from each other, eyes locked in battle.

She tips her glossy lips up. "Do you ever *not* sound like an uptight lawyer?"

I pretend to think about it while I shuffle. "No." I push the deck across the table and she splits it, then taps the stack on the left side. I tuck the right stack beneath the left, then deal us each seven cards before turning over the first card. A red seven. "Do you ever get that stick out of your ass?"

"Aw, Hall, you thinking about my ass?" she coos, not missing a beat. She slaps a green seven down.

I swallow and force my expression to remain neutral, pulling out a card to make her take four cards from the deck and tossing it onto the pile. "Nope." *Just like I'm not thinking about it right now.*

Not thinking about how glorious she'd look bent over, her plush ass in the air, sporting red welts from where I've spanked her.

Not thinking about her generous thighs, either, and how they'd feel around my ears.

Definitely not thinking about the way that sassy mouth of hers would look wrapped around my cock.

Absolutely none of these things have crossed my mind.

I am a God damn saint.

I'm also far too enthusiastic when I win the game, slapping my hands on the table as I jump up, whooping and jumping around like my team just won the national college football championship.

"Wow," Charlotte drawls. "You're every bit the exact type of winner I thought you'd be."

I preen. "You mean the *winning* kind?"

"I mean the obnoxious kind. No wonder you represent the people you do."

Whether she intends them to or not, her words hit their mark. In an instant, I've dropped my arms to my sides and clamped my mouth shut, putting the sweet "churn the butter" moves I was doing to rest.

Ten years isn't a long time in the lawyer world, and my success comes down to the fact that I didn't flinch when my clients made it clear that not only were they well aware of the impact they were having on people, they didn't give a shit, and further, the only way I was going to work for them was if I turned my ruthless determination to win at all costs into a weapon for their benefit. So I did, and I've been handsomely rewarded for it. The problem is, my ability to compartmentalize the shit I've seen and done, and still sleep at night, is getting pretty frayed.

Charlotte's pious stance doesn't help.

Wordlessly, I do a one-eighty and round the corner to the kitchen, a thin chute of a room the producers no doubt designed to be tight on purpose. There's no way two people can actually cook in here without constantly sliding past each other. I grab a beer from the fridge and pop it open, not caring that it's nowhere near lunchtime, chugging half while forcing my bad mood away and inspecting the food we've got to work with.

I'm no culinary master—my twin brother Ox is the better cook—but our parents made sure we learned enough to keep ourselves alive once we graduated. "Looks like we've got options for meals," I call.

There's no answer.

I try again. "You're not a vegan, right? As long as you're not vegan, I think we're good. Unless you're allergic to something really weird—"

"Why did you come on this show?" Charlotte leans against the door jamb, her soft arm flat against the glossy white paint.

For a second, I consider telling her the truth. Confessing everything to her and hoping she's the person who can wipe away my sins. Then I remember that we're being filmed, and she'll turn anything I say against me eventually.

"To ruin your chances at happiness, Counselor."

Her lips flatten into a line. Not a thin one—they're far too luscious for that—but a line nonetheless. She shakes her head and mutters, "You're such a dick."

I'm gracious enough to bow. "Why Charlotte, that might be the nicest thing you've ever said about me."

She lets out an aggrieved scowl and spins away.

I enjoy the view as she retreats.

CHAPTER 5

CHARLOTTE

YOU KNOW, FOR about five seconds there, I almost thought he was human. After I ribbed him about coming on the show, I saw something that resembled an actual emotion flit across his perfect face. It almost looked like…regret? Sadness?

Thankfully, he remedied that situation by opening his mouth. His gorgeous, stupid mouth.

I glare at the bookshelf with no books, then decide I can watch television. But when I look around, I realize there's no television.

No books, no television, and of course no phones. They took those away from us when we were still in our separate trailers, getting looked over and having our bags searched for contraband like we were about to go to prison.

Which, now that I'm stuck here with Levi, it kind of feels like jail. A relatively cushy jail that I get to escape after twenty-four hours, but still.

Knowing it's futile, but also unable to help myself, I walk to the bedroom to see if any books or a television are in there. Nothing at first glance, but surely there's stuff around here. The bed is definitely a king with a sturdy-looking headboard, covered in a plain white down comforter and pillows. The room is wide enough to accommodate small bedside tables on either side, so I check the one closest to me.

It's filled with condoms. All sizes, all flavors. I stifle a smile and close the drawer.

On the other side, I half expect to find a bible. Instead, there's lube…and a small notebook and pen.

Interesting.

Not really sure what the producers thought would happen that they needed to toss a notebook and pen into the mix, but whatever.

I check the chest of drawers, too, but they're utterly empty.

The ensuite bathroom doesn't fare much better. On the counter is fresh toothpaste and toothbrushes, plus some makeup remover, soap, lotion, and shampoo and conditioner. Beneath the sink is just as dull: toilet paper, unopened boxes of multi-size tampons and pads, and a hair dryer. I'm going to assume it was a woman who put this together, though, or the tampons wouldn't be here. Towels and washcloths are hanging on the rack, and the shower has one of those removable shower heads.

Unbidden, a vision of Levi and me in the shower flies into my head. My back to his front, while he angles the shower head between my legs.

"We really do need to figure out what we're eating."

I jump and spin, my hand on my chest, and glare. "Holy shit, Levi! Give a girl a warning, why don't you?" My heart is freaking galloping. Seriously, how does a man as big as him not make any noise when approaching?

The asshole has the nerve to smile. "Sorry."

"Oh, *now* you're being nice?" I scoff. "You plan on poisoning my food?"

He tilts his head. "With what? Pepper flakes?"

I bite my tongue. That was almost funny.

He steps into the room, reducing the already small area into something that's miniscule. Inches separate us. I despise him, yet I find I don't hate being this close.

Nothing makes sense.

He meets my eyes. "You checking for cameras?"

I study him. "You're really obsessed with finding the cameras, aren't you?"

He studies me back just as openly and lets me think about my question for a minute. It's a great tactic, and I file it away for use in future depositions.

"Yes," he finally says. "And don't tell me you aren't. We may not like each other, you and I, but we were trained to be like this. To assume no one is telling the whole truth. That everything is a competition. And to assume everyone is out to one-up us, so we have to stay one step ahead."

My eyes widen, and my stupid heart melts a little. "Damn," I whisper. "That's the saddest thing I've ever heard."

He shrugs. "Tell me I'm wrong."

"You're wrong," I shoot back. In my head, all I can think is, *who hurt you?*

"I'm right, and you know it."

"You're not right. What you are is far too cynical for someone your age."

He folds his arms. "Untrue."

"Oh, that's most definitely true. 'Assume no one is telling the whole truth' and 'Everything is a competition'? That's Grinch-level, Levi."

"I have two brothers," he counters with a shrug. "Besides, I must not be too far gone if I'm on this show."

"Tell me why you're here."

He steps closer and puts a hand on the wall, forcing me to look up at him if I don't want an up close and personal view of his starched white button-down. The move might be sexy if we weren't in the world's most boring bathroom. Then again, it *does* have that removable shower head...and really bright lighting. The bonus of which is that I'm treated to the show that is Levi Hall's incredibly expressive eyes. The ice blue of the irises remain, but they're ringed by navy and shot through with hints of turquoise and more navy. They narrow now as he contemplates me. "This isn't a deposition, Miss Kelly. In fact, aren't we supposed to be learning more about each other?"

"Precisely." I've got him right where I want him. "This is me trying to learn more about you. Why are you on the show?"

The air crackles with tension, neither one of us backing down. I'm surrounded by him, literally and figuratively, and I swear his scent is like a damn drug. It feels like being snuggled up in the winter. For all I know, it's just deodorant and clothing detergent, but whatever it is, it works on him.

Way too effectively.

He still doesn't speak, and I've stopped breathing deeply. I'm choosing to believe that it's to ensure my tits don't hit his massive, mountain-man-with-an-axe level chest.

When it's clear he is not going to answer, I duck under his arm—an arm that's probably as big as my thighs, and my thighs aren't skinny—and don't bother looking back. As I leave the bathroom, I launch my latest barb. "I learned everything I needed to know about you in law school, Levi. And your abhorrent clients have only confirmed it."

Chapter 6

LEVI

DAMN THIS WOMAN.

I had her exactly where I wanted her, and I was *this* close to leaning down and giving her the kiss of her life. Then she had to go and open her infuriating mouth.

Not bothering to keep my eyes off her ass as she leaves, I ask, "What's that supposed to mean?"

She doesn't answer.

I follow her through the bedroom and into the hallway, then keep going as she makes her way back to the living room. "Charlotte."

"What?" Her voice is loud as she whirls back to me, glossy dark brown hair swinging as she throws her hands in the air. The move is calculated and meant to throw me off my game, but she should know better than that. It'll take way more than this.

I repeat the question. "What do you mean, you learned all there was to know about me in law school?"

She jerks her head back. "You can't be serious."

"Deadly."

"I mean," she seethes, closing the distance as she stalks to me and lands her finger on my chest, "that you're an entitled, rich, spoiled, self-absorbed jerk who talks over women like it's his God-given right." She jabs her nail in. "You're a cheat and a sore loser," *jab*, "*and* you were a complete drunkard every single Homecoming," *jab*, "who thought you were too important to be bothered to wear the morning coats and ties like the rest of us!"

I've let her back me against an actual wall, and her hazel eyes are nearly green with rage as her body shakes with gloriously beautiful—though entirely misplaced—anger.

She's stunning, and thank God for the wall that's holding me up right now.

She's also dead wrong.

"No," I say softly, reaching up to gently remove her finger from where it's practically embedded itself into my pec. "But let's unwrap all of that, shall we?"

She makes a noise in the back of her throat.

"That wasn't a yes, but it wasn't a no—so I'll take it." I take a moment to gather my thoughts, grateful that she's allowing me to do so. Then I hold up a finger. "First, that I'm entitled, rich, and spoiled."

"Prove me wrong," she says, spitting my own words back at me.

I grin, but it's not even that satisfying. "I grew up with an older brother and a twin brother. My dad was a public high school chemistry teacher, and my mom made it through two years of undergrad before she got pregnant with my oldest brother. Me and my twin followed soon after. She never finished school. Never held a job outside the home. We were dirt poor." I hold up another finger. "I'm also from a small town on the beach called Lucky, Alabama. My twin and I were scrawny as hell and got picked on mercilessly by our brother and everybody in school. Until the summer before high school. Suddenly, we were huge. Mom shoved us into football because she didn't know what else to do. Woman spent half her days feeding us for a while. You ever played football, Charlotte?"

She shakes her head.

"Softball? Basketball? Any team sport?"

"I run."

I consider her answer. "That tracks. Solitary, no one to push you but yourself…"

"And where I come up with my best ideas, *Counselor*," she says, raising an unimpressed eyebrow. "Not that you'd know a novel trial tactic if it came up and introduced itself to you."

I ignore that particular dagger. "There's a lot to be said about learning how to play with others. To getting laid out, flat on your back, over and over again, by someone bigger than you. To being out*run* by someone faster than you. To understanding that you may be special to your parents, but on the field, you're replaceable."

"What about the quarterback?"

The sass on this woman. I tip my chin. "Have a good look at me, Charlotte. I wasn't the quarterback."

She takes the invitation, raking her eyes over me slowly. I feel every second of her perusal. I know what I look like to most people: a giant meathead in a monkey suit with shit for brains. But Charlotte knows what my brain is actually capable of, and it makes the way her breathing slows that much more arousing.

She licks her lips. "Looks pretty good to me."

It takes all of my control to keep from pushing her against the wall and kissing her senseless.

Instead, I smirk. Because I need every ounce of self-control against her. Anyone else and I'd be happily working to convince them I was worthy of a longer-term thing—that *is* the entire point of this show, after all. But all bets were off the second I laid eyes on Charlotte.

I hold up a third finger. "'Complete drunkard every Homecoming.' That, Miss Kelly, is absolutely correct. You're also aware that it was the standard for every single one of us."

"A standard you were more than happy to lower yourself to."

I sigh. "Charlotte. The entire point of our shenanigans on Homecoming was to be little shits. You know the history. Law students wanted to wear morning coats for the game, but were told they could only wear them in the morning. So they decided to begin the day at the crack of dawn, in said morning coats, and got drunker than goats." I grin broadly. "And thus, a tradition was born."

With a roll of her eyes, she waves at a corner camera. "You wanna give the audience an explanation of what a morning coat is?"

"A fancy coat with tails. What's that Netflix show you ladies like—Bridgerton? Like that. Only black or gray. With a button down and a cravat."

She crosses her arms, her eyes bright with mirth. "Now tell me why you never wore one."

I close my eyes. I walked right into it. This is how she wins. She distracts me, then goes in for the kill. Still, I'd planned on addressing it, so no time like the present. I flop onto the couch and kick my dress shoes off, extending my legs over the cushions to make sure I take up all the room. "Comfy. You'll enjoy sleeping out here."

She growls. It's incredibly enjoyable *and* erotic, but I ignore the erotic part of it.

"Because, Counselor. You'll recall my previous statement about being poor?"

She lifts a shoulder. "I was poor, Levi. You didn't see me shirking tradition."

I bite the inside of my cheek and narrow my eyes. "Trailer park poor?"

"No—" she starts.

I cut her off. "Then there's the difference, Charlotte. I grew up in a trailer park. I'm not ashamed of it, either. It was a damn nice trailer, and my parents did the absolute best they could raising us. So, the morning coats. There weren't any big enough for me to rent, and I sure as shit wasn't going to buy one."

She opens her mouth to retort, then closes it.

"Finally rendered you speechless?" I laugh humorlessly. "Glad it took repeatedly telling you I barely had two nickels to rub together to finally shut you up."

The thing is, all this is doing is making me want her that much more. And thinking about all the other ways I'd love to render her speechless. Learning how she tastes is chief among them.

CHAPTER 7

CHARLOTTE

"I SUPPOSE NOW you're going to use that same argument to explain why you talk over women?" It's the only response I've got, and I don't like the metaphorical corner he's got me backed into.

"Have I talked over you at all while we've been here?"

"No."

"What about in court?"

I shake my head.

He shifts, getting even cozier in that couch. Have I mentioned the asshole is built like a tank? And his legs in those dress pants...God *damn*. "Then where is this coming from?"

"Law school, Hall. I told you everything I needed to know about you I learned in law school. I know you were listening."

He blinks. "Okay. That's been a decade. You're going to need to give me a hint here."

I swerve. "Why are you on this show?"

"Why are *you* on this show?" he retorts.

"This isn't a cross-examination."

"Isn't it?" He shifts again, adjusting his hips and drawing my attention to his crotch and what appears to be a rather impressive package. I snap my eyes back to his face. His full lips tip up in satisfaction. He stretches then, raising his arms up and arching his back so his button-down strains at the seams, the fabric between pearl buttons opening just enough to hint at the skin beneath and really give me a thirst trap of a show. He settles his arms on the back and side of the couch, fully aware of what he's done, and judging by his smile, incredibly pleased with himself. "Come on, Char. I'm curious. Why are you here? And feel free to explain why you wore that while you're at it." He flicks his fingers over my outfit as he speaks.

I look down at my dark wash jeans and emerald-green blouse. They're nothing I'd wear to hang out in a house for twenty-four hours, but I may or may not have donned some shape wear, and if, say, I *was* wearing what is essentially a girdle, then I'd need the jeans and blouse to cover the evidence. I'm not ashamed of my body, but I have to assume a size eighteen looks a little fluffy on camera. Why not use every tool at my disposal? I meet his eyes. "What's wrong with my outfit, Mr. Business Suit?"

"Oh, but you like my suit," he murmurs seductively.

My mouth dries, and I curse inwardly. I don't need him acting all sexy and broody. It's bad enough that I want to ride his face like a roller coaster and feel his auburn beard scrape against my thighs. I don't need him putting a gruff voice to the fantasy. "Irrelevant."

His eyes spark with delight. "Did I just win? I think I won."

I look to the ceiling, praying for patience. "Why are you here, Levi?"

"You first."

I heave a sigh and walk to the lone chair, settling myself in it and realizing too late that I can't really breathe at this angle. But I'm committed, so I stay put. "You know what our lives are like. You know how hard it is to meet someone. I thought that this might, I don't know, jumpstart something special." I don't meet his eyes the entire time I speak.

"And I'm not special?"

I snort. "Be serious, Levi."

He levels his gaze on me. "I'm always serious, Charlotte."

Butterflies erupt in my stomach, and I swat them away. They have absolutely no business being here. I take a breath. "Fine. You're serious. So am I. This is me trying to make good on a promise I made. And, it feels like…it feels like I'm running out of time, okay?"

He looks at me quizzically. "You're thirty-five."

"Exactly." I don't want to think about what it means that he knew exactly how old I was. We were in law school together. It's an educated guess on his part and no more. That has to be it.

"So?"

I groan. "Levi. *So* it means that I'm old. What if I want kids? What if I want a marriage?"

He shrugs. "Then have them."

I want to shake him. "You know, for as pretty as you are, you're really stupid."

A shadow of something flits across his face, but it's gone in an instant. "You think I'm pretty?"

"You *know* you're pretty. I'm not saying anything earth-shattering here."

He winks. "Maybe. But getting you to say something about me that's even remotely positive? I don't know, Charlotte. Feels like another win." His lips tip up slightly.

I roll my eyes. "Your turn."

He hesitates. "Honestly?"

"That's sort of why we're here, Hall. Honesty. Or did you stop thinking about ethics the second we left law school? Because your clients—"

"Are just as worthy of defense as the next person," he finishes.

The *scoff* I scoff. Crossing my arms—and not missing how his eyes flick down to my breasts and back to my face—I say, "Your clients are the reason our society is going to shit. Corporations thinking they can just waltz around, swinging their dicks all over the place and doing whatever the hell they want to the people unfortunate enough to work for them."

He smirks. "You thinking about my dick, Charlotte?"

Oh, that asshole. Heat rises in my face, and I clap back. "In your dreams. Answer the question."

"Fine. I'm here because I'm lonely."

I open my mouth to retort, but then my brain actually processes the words he said. And *now* he's the asshole. This mother fucker just laid himself bare for me and the damn world while lounging in an impeccably tailored button down.

His hand—big, with thick fingers—flexes against the back of the couch, bringing every fantasy I have ever had about him roaring to life. He was always good looking in law school, but his hair has darkened to a deep auburn, and now he's sporting that fucking beard. It takes him from good looking to downright sexy, forcing my attention to his hooded turquoise eyes and the expressive eyebrows above them.

He chuckles knowingly now. "You weren't ready for that level of honesty from me, were you? Seems I keep winning here. Maybe all it took was putting us on a reality show for me to finally get beneath that exterior of yours."

I blink. "And what exterior is that?"

"Oh, come on now," he cajoles, his voice low. "You know precisely how you present yourself to the world. It's never changed. Sure, you're more polished now, and that's to be expected. But at your core? You're the same woman you were back then."

I can barely breathe, and I don't know if it's because I'm waiting to hear what he'll say or if it's this damn shape wear. "You going to tell the audience what kind of woman I supposedly was, Hall?"

He shifts, putting his feet on the floor and leaning forward to put his elbows on his knees. When he meets my eyes, they're dead earnest. "The kind who, despite my best efforts, never left my mind. The kind who knew every answer the professors put in front of her, and made me work my ass off in a vain effort to be even *half* as smart as her. The kind who, God help me, is even more lethal now than she ever was back then."

CHAPTER 8

CHARLOTTE

IT'S OFFICIAL: I can't breathe. And it's not the shape wear.

I'm more *lethal*? What the hell does that even mean?

And the look he's giving me right now? Holy hell.

I lean forward to grab the water that has miraculously appeared out of what feels like thin air. After a sip, I meet his eyes again. I don't even remember what we were talking about. Do I tell him that? Or do I just change the subject?

I change the subject. Definitely.

"Tell me something, Levi."

His thick eyebrow raises. Fucking everything about him is thick. His cock is guaranteed to be just as ruinous, I bet.

But I'm not going to worry about his cock, because it's not getting anywhere near me.

Is that true?

Yeah, that might not be true.

Shit. Was that really water? Is the wine finally hitting me? Isn't the point of these shows to keep us drunk?

"Still waiting on what you want me to tell you, Charlotte."

Even his voice is thick. Which, I know, makes no sense, but here we are. I need to get myself back on an even keel.

"How did it feel the first time you lost a case to me?"

He blinks, and I know I've hit a sore spot. Good. Because whatever this is? It needs to stop.

"Are we being honest?" he asks.

I nod. "Seems like a good course of action."

He drops his head, a behemoth at rest. I gulp air in, eager for oxygen now that I'm not staring into his eyes. With his head still down, he answers. "I hated losing. Before that case, I'd never lost so much as a motion. Then you showed up and annihilated me." He looks up, his irises dark with emotion. "But you deserved the win."

Instinctively, I can tell there's more he wants to say. But he won't.

"Though I hated the look on my associate's face, as though his hero had just gotten shot."

I smirk. "You're not a superhero, Levi."

He holds my gaze. He's fucking relentless. "Never said I was."

I look around for a clock before remembering there isn't one. "What time do you think it is?"

"Why? You ready to escape me already?"

My lips curve. "Did you just make a joke?"

He shrugs.

I laugh. "You did. Good job, Levi. Maybe there's hope for you yet."

He rolls his eyes and stands. "Come on. Let me feed you."

I don't appreciate the way my stomach flutters in response. I'm going to pretend it's because I'm just hungry, and not that it has anything to do with the fact that no man has ever talked about feeding me. None of them have ever talked about food much at all, now that I think about it.

I rise and follow him, still unable to keep my eyes off his butt.

"Don't you want to put something more comfortable on?" I blurt.

He stops and turns. "Why, Charlotte, are you trying to get me to take my clothes off?" His eyes glitter with mirth.

I feel my cheeks heat. "I just—seems like a suit isn't the most comfortable thing to be wearing, that's all."

Lazily, his gaze travels from the top of my body to my toes and back, setting me on fire. "Seems like you could use getting comfortable, too."

"I—"

He waves a hand at me. "You're wearing shape wear under there, right?"

I gape. "How the hell can you know that?"

He levels me with a heated look. "Because I *know* what you look like, Charlotte."

I can't decide if I should be flattered or mortified.

He takes a step toward me. "Tell you what. We'll both change into something more comfortable, and then you'll let me feed you."

Jesus. Did they make it hotter in here? They did. They probably want us gallivanting about in our undies and little else. Even still, I swallow and nod. "Sure." My traitorous voice cracks.

He gives a wolfish grin. "You go first."

I turn without a word and leave, making sure the bedroom door shuts firmly behind me. The whimper that leaves my mouth can't be helped. That man. I hate him.

Right?

Shaking my head, I grab my overnight bag and pull out my favorite pair of yoga pants, along with a lacy bralette that doesn't hold my tits up for shit but looks awfully pretty, and an oversize tee. I no longer care what I look like. I just need to be able to *breathe.*

Although, if Levi keeps looking at me that way, it won't matter what I'm wearing.

After changing, I make my way to the tiny kitchen and see

Levi surveying the fridge with a thoughtful expression. "Your turn."

He turns, and I get the absolute joy of watching him take me in. It's…powerful. Because his jaw slackens for a millisecond, his eyes going hazy, and I can see what he might look like if I were riding him like the horse he almost certainly is in bed.

He recovers so quickly that if I weren't paying attention, I would have missed the entire thing. "Right."

I don't bother moving out of his way this time, and I catch his scent once more as he brushes past me. Fuck me. He is all man. Upon reflection, I've decided that he smells like a Christmas tree forest. Does that make any sense at all, given that I'd swear he was the personification of the Grinch? No. No, it does not. But there we have it.

I barely have time to refill my water before he reappears, and thank God for it, because my mouth goes as dry as the Sahara.

Levi Hall is wearing gray sweatpants.

With…*holy mother of*…no underwear.

Is it hot in here? It's hot in here.

I rake my eyes up from the impressive situation happening inside those divine sweatpants and take in the thin white tee he wears. His arms are inked in colorful sleeve tattoos. Tattoos I had no idea he had, because of how meticulously they're placed. Which makes sense, because for as common as they are these days, I can promise you if a judge got even a peek of one, Levi would be immediately on the defense.

But enough of thinking about Levi in the courtroom. Because the Levi standing in front of me is…

"You okay, Charlotte?" The bastard smirks at me, knowing full well the effect he's having.

I sniff and straighten. "I'm fine."

Totally fine. But I've gotta be honest here: I'm going to need some serious help in the self-preservation department for the next however many hours.

"Good." He breezes past me again, and I call upon my waning willpower to keep my eyes off the way his dick moves as he walks.

Nope. No willpower. None. She gone. Poof. Into the wind.

"Sausage?"

I nearly choke. "What?"

He laughs. "I said, there's some breakfast food in here if you want me to make that. Eggs, biscuits, sausage."

Twenty-four hours might kill me.

CHAPTER 9

LEVI

HER CHEEKS HEAT and I keep laughing. I knew exactly what I was doing when I put this outfit on, and I knew what I was doing when I said sausage.

She's never like this. She is definitely not in work mode, and I gotta say: I like this version of Charlotte.

The other version of Charlotte? The one where she eviscerates me in front of my clients and judges?

That version is hot as hell, too.

She stammers. "Sausage. Yes. I'd like that."

I double down. "How many?"

Her eyes jerk to mine, her cheeks growing rosier by the second. "How many...sausages?"

"Yep."

"Oh. Um, two. No—three. Well—one? Two." She grows more and more flustered as I lean against the stove, folding my arms and enjoying the show.

"How about four?" I prod. "I bet you can take four."

She narrows her eyes. "You're doing this on purpose."

I bark out a laugh, unable to take it anymore. "Hell yes I am."

And wouldn't you know it? She laughs right along with me.

And it hits me right in the chest. The urge, the absolute need, to make her laugh again and again, is almost unbearable.

"Scoot over," she says, still smiling and shaking her head. "I don't think you can be trusted with my sausage."

I snort and make room for her in the kitchen. The very tiny kitchen. The tiny kitchen so tiny that we can't help but brush past each other as we put together a meal, her luscious body nearly undoing all my willpower with every *excuse me* and *um, sorry* she murmurs. By the time we're done, I've watched her dice a tomato like a pro, and she's complimented my egg whisking skills.

It's damn near domestic, and between it and my growing need to feel the heat of her beneath me, I'm almost freaked out.

Except that's why I signed up for this damn show. Her, too.

"My eggs are better than yours," she says as she chews.

I raise a brow at the declaration. After I finish a bite, I set my fork down. "Thank you."

She studies me. "Thank you?"

"For making certain I know exactly where I stand with you. I'd hate to forget that you detest me."

Her eyes flare. "I don't detest you."

"No?"

"No."

"Then please enlighten me." And yes, here again, I'm well aware of what I'm doing. I've got about nineteen hours, give or take, to make this move in one direction or the other. And, God help me, I think I know which direction I want it to go in. What I *don't* know is if she's willing to go there with me.

"I've already told you how I feel about you."

"No, you haven't. You've told me you learned all you needed to know about me in law school. What was it again? I'm privileged, spoiled, and—"

"Fine," she interrupts with a sigh. "You're...different than I expected."

I'd like a reward for how I don't pump my fist in victory. "And how's that?"

"You're enjoying this way too much," she accuses.

"I am," I admit with a smile.

She contemplates me. "For one thing, you're much more… honest than I thought you would be."

Interesting. I wait on the rest.

"And the tattoos." Her cheeks flush as she allows herself to look at them more closely. "I did not see those coming."

"Not many do."

"They're beautiful." Her hazel eyes meet mine and hold, and I get the distinct impression that she might be talking about more than the tattoos right now.

"Thank you. Do you have any?"

"Nah. Love the idea of it, but haven't ever thought of anything that I want on my body permanently."

"Once I started, I didn't want to stop."

"Clearly." Her eyes stray back to my arms, taking in the different sleeves. They're filled with flowers, water, animals. All of them incredibly symbolic and personal. "Any particular meaning behind them?"

I'm overcome by the urge to confess that each one is, in its own way, an apology to the planet, and the people whose lives I made worse by the cases I won. But there's no way I'll admit that. Certainly not in front of the cameras. Instead, I flash her a carefree smile and shrug. "Not really. Just let the tattoo artist do their thing, for the most part."

She doesn't believe me. It's as clear as day. But she doesn't push, and for that, I'm grateful.

We finish our meal, then work together to clean up. I excuse myself to brush my teeth, only to find her pulling out her own toiletry kit when I return to the bedroom to put mine away.

She smiles. "I have to brush my teeth after every meal; I don't like the taste to linger."

"Same," I agree.

She joins me in the living room a few minutes later, and my eyes can't behave. I don't bother trying to be a gentleman anymore, either, letting my gaze roam her body appreciatively.

She flushes under the attention, but gives it right back to me. I pat the couch.

She comes and sits, choosing to sit as far away from me as possible. But that's okay. I can work with this.

"Give me your feet."

She raises a perfect eyebrow. "You got a thing for feet, Counselor?"

I chuckle. "No. But even if I did, then would it really be a problem?"

She thinks about it, then smiles. "Nah." She pulls her feet up and I guide them into my lap.

I take a foot and peel the sock off, taking a moment to appreciate the candy red polish on her pale toes, then begin to massage. Her eyes roll back in her head and the groan she issues is absolutely a turn-on, low and breathy.

"Holy shit," she moans. "That feels amazing."

"I know."

"Cocky motherfucker," she says, but there's no heat behind it like there was earlier.

"Your feet are tiny and my hands are huge—it's not like this is hard, Charlotte. Of course it feels good."

"Shh, don't speak. You're ruining it." She closes her eyes and lets her head fall back, and I take the opportunity to really study her.

The years have taken their toll on her, same as they do on anyone, but she's all the more beautiful for it. Gone is the wide-eyed innocence that she had in law school; now those eyes, when they're open, are shrewd and calculating in one moment, and soft and kind the next. Her body is plush and generous, the kind I'd fucking kill to feel beneath me and on top of me. Massive tits, a belly and hips to sink my fingers and teeth into, and thighs that I haven't stopped thinking about having wrapped around my head as I fuck her with my tongue. Her hair is just as mesmerizing, falling in thick caramel waves to just below her shoulder. Plenty for me to grab on to when her own mouth is wrapped around my cock.

I want to grab onto every part of her. There isn't one part of her that's thin or skinny, and thank fucking God for it.

I knead deeper, and she issues yet another moan. "Tell me what you want," I urge.

"Keep doing that, but higher. Get right above the toes. Just like that. Yes," she hisses quietly.

And immediately I'm hard.

She feels it beneath her other foot, too, and opens one hazel eye to grin wickedly at me. "What's going on down there?"

I grab her other foot and start massaging it. "You know exactly what's going on."

Her other eye opens as she blatantly assesses me. "Not going to try and deny anything?"

I press a thumb into the arch of her foot. "Why would I deny it? I have a gorgeous woman in my hands and she's making noises that make me wonder what she'd sound like in bed. Of course I'm a little hard."

Her smile broadens. "A little hard? That's a little?"

Now it's my turn to smile wickedly. "Yes, Charlotte. That's a little."

"Color me impressed."

"You have no idea."

She laughs again, and God, it sounds so good. "Tell me why you didn't take any of the big jobs after law school. I know you were offered the same ones as me. "

"So this is your ruse, huh? Get me soft by plying me with a foot massage and then go in for the kill?" Her eyes sparkle as she says it.

Jesus. I'm talking about eyes sparkling? I'm ridiculous.

"You don't have to answer. I just assumed I'd be working next to you or across the courtroom from you pretty quickly. But you fell off the face of the earth after school."

She's quiet while she assesses me, then seems to decide something. "My mom got sick. My family needed me, so I did what I needed to do."

"And when you reappeared?"

She looks away and gathers herself, then meets my gaze. "Mom passed away. Breast cancer. Fought it as long as she could, and it spread. There was no getting her back after that."

The shock of her words spears right through me. "Charlotte, I'm so sorry."

She smiles softly. "Thank you. Me, too. But after that, I knew I needed to get back to what I loved. I worked the whole time, obviously, but it wasn't until after she passed away that I took the gig that got me across from you in that courtroom."

"Shocked the hell out of me."

"How? Didn't you see my name on the pleadings?"

My jaw pops and I smile ruefully. "That's what associates are for, Charlotte."

She chuckles. "Of course. Big and bad Levi Hall can't be bothered with the minutiae. He just parachutes in right before the big day."

I trace the line of her calf with my fingers, marveling at how damn soft her skin is, before admitting, "That's...incredibly accurate."

She cackles. "There you go. Honesty looks good on you, Hall."

"You know what else would look good on me?"

"I swear to god, if you say—"

"You."

Her face flushes even as she laughs. "You went there, didn't you?"

I use her legs to pull her towards me, throwing her off balance just enough that I'm able to haul her onto my lap.

Her expressive eyes heat instantly. When I wrap my arms around her and let my hands go to her ass, they darken.

"Yes. I went there. And then I did this." I slide my hands up and down her ass, wishing like hell she was naked.

She nods, licking her lower lip as her hands move up to my neck. Her nails lightly scrape at the skin, enough to make me close my eyes for a second.

"I still don't think I like you very much," she whispers.

I open my eyes to meet hers. "I don't know I believe that."

She hums.

"But even if you do, is that going to change what's about to happen here?"

"What exactly to you think is about to happen here?" But as she says it, she leans closer. The heat of her center is right over my cock, and her breasts aren't even an inch from my chest.

"I can tell you what I want to happen, and then you can tell me if you agree with that."

Her nail goes in circles at the nape of my neck. "Okay."

I lower my voice, not at all interested in letting the mics pick up my words. "First, I want to kiss the hell out of you. Then, I want to make you come. First with my mouth, and then then with my cock. The kiss can happen here or in the bedroom, but the rest is absolutely happening in there, because that's where no cameras are."

CHAPTER 10

CHARLOTTE

HOLY MOTHERFORKING FORKBALLS. He really went there.

And I am here for it.

He watches me expectantly, waiting to see what my reaction is. Meanwhile, his cock is rock hard beneath me, and all I want to do is let him ravish me and do exactly what he said he'd do. The way he's looking at me, like I'm a meal and he's a starving man, is so foreign that I'm not sure what to do with it.

I don't know the last time a man looked at me like he actually wanted me. My last few boyfriends, if you can even call them that, were more like guys I could call if I really just needed some dick. They serviced me and that was about it. It wasn't love—not even close.

And I'm not saying what Levi is giving me is love. I don't know him well enough for that. But the look in his eyes? There's more there than just a tolerance of me. There's desire.

It's hot as fuck.

"So, Charlotte," he murmurs. "What's it going to be?"

I grab for the last bit of control I have. "You can try."

"I can try…what?"

"You can try to make me come. It's not easy."

His eyes darken. "You're saying I'm going to have to put in the work?"

My core fucking melts. "That's what I'm saying."

His grin is wicked. "Charlotte, if there's one thing about me that you should know, it's that I am relentless. I'm not afraid of putting in the effort. Especially if that effort involves making you come." He leans up, his mouth hovering just below mine. It's clear he's letting me have all the control, but I have no doubt that he'll take the reins the second I consent.

Am I ready for this? I mean, I came on this insane show for a connection, and this is certainly a connection. Is it one that I want to pursue after the twenty-four hours are up? That, I can't speak to.

But what I *can* do is let this fine-ass man have his way with me.

"Kiss me, Hall."

He strikes, his lips meeting mine with a ferocity that takes my breath away. Immediately I feel as though I've walked into the best kind of trap, as his hands tighten around me and he pulls me to him.

I go willingly, settling farther onto his lap and feeling the way his cock reacts, pressing against the thin fabric of my pants. I couldn't be happier that I'm not wearing panties.

His hand grips my hair and angles my head so he can kiss me better. His tongue skates along the seam of my lips, and I open for him, forcing myself to hold back the groan as he deepens the kiss.

Holy fuck, this man can kiss. And if this is how he uses his tongue in my mouth? Yes, please. Yes to all of it.

I shift, the ache between my legs already heavy with want.

"You want more?" he murmurs against my lips.

"Yes."

He scoots us to the edge of the couch, and I go to stand. But his hands grip my thighs. "Where the fuck are you going?" he growls. He fucking *growls*.

"I was—"

He tightens his grip and stands, lifting me easily. "I just got my hands on you, Charlotte. No way am I letting go."

I gasp as his mouth meets mine again, his beard soft on my skin as his mouth takes me into freaking space.

Holy shit. The way this man kisses. It's with his whole body, the way he pulls me to him with each stroke of his tongue, his hands gripping my legs solidly. The same feeling from earlier floods me: Safety. Home.

None of it makes sense, but I'm not in the mood to dissect it like it's an opening statement.

Though, as far as opening statements go, this kiss is absolutely winning. Fuck me.

"Kind of hoping you let me, Charlotte." He grins as he spins us in the direction of the bedroom.

"Did I say that out loud?" My face heats.

"You did." His gaze shifts to a corner in the ceiling, then back to me. "I think the camera's gotten everything it needs, don't you?"

I nod vigorously, hitching myself up to ease the ache between my legs. I need pressure.

He reads me like a book. "Coming right up," he murmurs against my neck. "Just a few more steps."

He carries me into the bedroom and kicks the door shut.

I can't help but giggle. "You know they're going to love that move in the editing room."

He wiggles his eyebrows. "Why do you think I did it?"

Now I laugh, but it's smothered by his lips on mine once more. He releases my legs and I slide down his massive body, holding myself up by my arms around his neck. When my toes hit the floor, I stay tipped up on them, not wanting to lose the connection we have.

He reads me again, moving us the few steps to the bed and turning so it's his ass that hits the mattress. He guides me onto his lap again, and I melt against him.

"These muscles, holy fuck, Levi. What do you do to look like this?"

His grin is absolutely filthy. "Wouldn't you like to know?" He slides his hands beneath my shirt and has it off in one smooth motion, his mouth dipping between my breasts. He inhales.

"Fuck, you smell good," he breathes. "Whatever it is, it's phenomenal."

I arch my back to give him better access. "Just soap and me." I moan as he slips one of the bralette straps off and captures a nipple in his mouth and sucks.

I swivel my hips in time with his tongue. His amazing, glorious tongue.

He moves to the other and I take the second he gives me to pull his shirt off, and I nearly choke on air.

The man is a tatted up, auburn-haired and bearded Henry Cavill and I am fucking *here* for it. I look up to the ceiling and send a prayer of thanks to whomever is clearly looking out for me.

His chest is solid muscle, each pec so defined that it takes everything I have not to slam him on his back and start licking every divot and plane on him.

God bless this man's genetics and sense of, I don't know, duty to himself? Whatever it is, I am grateful.

"I take it you like what you see."

I jerk my eyes to his and find nothing but amusement in there. "Have you seen yourself?" I counter. "How does anyone not like what they see?"

He shrugs. "You'd be surprised."

"Yeah, actually, I would. You're a fucking gift to behold, Levi. I have no idea what I did to deserve such a treat, but I'm real happy about it."

He laughs, a deep belly laugh that I feel all the way to my toes. "Come here," he says softly, pulling my mouth to his once again.

We kiss for I don't even know how long, going from sweet to heated to sweet again. Finally, he shifts us, pulling my bralette all the way off and looking at my leggings.

"I want those off," he states.

I start pulling them off.

"And then I want you on my face."

I stop. "I'm sorry—what?"

"I want those delicious thighs to be my earmuffs. And I want to bury my tongue inside your pussy."

Holy. *Shit.*

I have never divested myself of my clothes faster in my life. His satisfied grin as he lies down and I straddle his chest is almost enough to make me come right then and there, but then the man goes and licks his fucking lips like I'm about to be the best thing he's ever tasted.

And sure, this might typically be where I stop and ask a partner if they're sure, because I'm not a small woman next to most people. But right now, my knees barely hit the mattress as I make my way up his chest. And when his arms encircle my thighs and pull me down to his face, I lose all sense of self.

"Fuck, Charlotte," he whispers. "I have fantasized about this for so long. Look at your pretty pussy." Then he goes to town, licking my seam and dipping his tongue between my folds, sucking on my clit.

I grip the headboard and cry out, the feel of him so much better than it has any right to be.

His hands dig into my thighs in response as he moans beneath me. "Ride my face, Charlotte."

"That might be the hottest thing anyone has ever said to me," I grit out, then proceed to do exactly what the man commanded. I ride his face like his mouth was made for my pussy. Like his tongue was made for my clit.

"You taste so good," he says. "You gonna come for me? Come all over my face like a good girl?"

"I told you; I don't come that easily."

He chuckles, his fingers digging into my flesh. "Liar."

I jerk my hips, my entire world centered on this man's filthy mouth and the things he's doing to me with it. Again and again I shift my hips, his tongue performing some kind of magic. "Fuck," I pant. "I'm going to—"

Right as I start to crest, he spanks me, delivering a punishing crack that sends me over the edge with a yell that I swear has never come out of me. My entire body convulses with the orgasm, and below me, Levi sucks and licks and nips at me, pulling me through.

When the bliss finally recedes, I raise up and fall over to the mattress, giggling like a schoolgirl.

"Holy shit, Levi. I have never—" I stop and simply let out a laugh.

He grins at me. "That wasn't even hard." His cockiness knows no bounds, but right now? He's fucking earned it. He raises up and looks down at me, taking me in with a hunger I have never had directed my way. "You are gorgeous, Charlotte. Absolutely stunning."

I've got a pretty face. I've always been told that. Usually in that delightful way that people have: "Your face is so pretty! It's a shame…" As if me having curves is something to be ashamed of. And I'm not. Having a belly and thighs and all the other things hasn't ever bothered me. But I'd be lying if I said I'd always wanted to know what it must feel like to be looked at with primal desire and want and need.

And right now? The way Levi is looking at me is fulfilling all those desires and then some.

He runs a hand over his face. "Seriously. Look at you. How no one has snatched you up and made you theirs is a Goddamn mystery."

"Take your pants off, Hall."

He tilts his lips up. "You ready for some sausage?"

I laugh and grab a pillow to throw at him. "I can't believe you said that earlier!"

"I had to!" he laughs. "You were staring at me like I was a piece of meat, so I went with it."

I go up on my knees and meet him in the middle of the bed, finally getting my hands on his substantial chest.

It's just as glorious as I thought it would be, and if I'm being honest, having it connected to the man who eats pussy like a champion just makes it that much better. I lean to kiss his chest, inhaling his warm Christmas tree scent as I do, then skating my hand down to rid him of the gray sweatpants. They pool at his knees, and together we move so that they're off.

"Relax," I instruct.

He does what I ask, propping himself up on the pillows and crossing his fingers behind his head. He's the very picture of debauched fantasies, a giant of a man, perfectly formed in thick, taut lines. His arms are a riot of color, popping against the white of the pillows and standing out in the expanse of his skin. I ogle him shamelessly, appreciating the comfort he has in his own body and how it gives me permission to be just as comfortable. Reaching out, I trace the heavy indent that leads from his pelvis to his cock, which is just as substantial as the rest of him. On a normal man, it'd be huge. But on Levi, it's simply proportional.

But yeah: huge.

I ain't mad about it.

"Thank you."

His body shakes as he laughs, his eyes bright as he asks, "You're welcome?"

I nod as I straddle him, then lean down to kiss him, reveling in how perfect it feels to have his large hands cup my ass.

"Pretty sure I'm the one who should be thanking you," he murmurs against my lips. "Because this ass, Charlotte. It was prominent in my law school fantasies, and while I managed to shove you out of my head for the years you weren't around, they came roaring back the second you wiped the floor with me in that first case."

I preen under the praise. "Yeah?"

"Yeah," he says affectionately.

My heart squeezes and I promptly ignore it. And then promptly stop ignoring it. I want this, and I don't want this, but I think if I wanted this with anyone, it might be the man under me, despite his questionable clients.

I shake my head. I've been befuddled by an orgasm. And by the fucking *specimen* I'm staring at. That I need to focus on, because the man deserves all my attention.

I kiss my way down his chest, licking every line I come to, delighting in the way his breath hitches with every swoop of my tongue. "Are you ticklish?"

He huffs out a tense laugh. "Not exactly? But a little."

"That's beyond adorable." I don't stop my path, switching to kisses for the line leading to his cock, feeling him relax beneath me.

"No tongue, just lips. Got it," I tease, settling between his legs and scraping my nails up and down his thick leg muscles.

He groans. "Oh my God, what are you doing?"

I grin. "Just giving you leg scratches."

His cock bobs deliciously in front of me, the tip of it beading with precum. "Whatever it is, it's heaven and you have to do it always."

I don't bother answering. Instead, I lean down to lick him,

starting at the base and swirling my tongue up to the tip, licking the precum and lifting my eyes to meet his.

"Never mind," he bites out, his voice rough. "I take it back. You can do whatever the fuck you want."

I grab his balls. "That's the right attitude." I continue my exploration of him, licking him up and down until he's a quivering mess, then taking him all the way into my mouth. I can't take him all the way to the back of my throat, and now isn't the time to try, so my hand makes up for the difference. The man isn't Pringles can large or anything insane like that, but unless I feel like choking, he's not going to feel the heat of my mouth at the base of his cock.

And considering the grunts and groans and tiny bits of praise he's dishing out above me, I think he's fine with that.

"Fuck, Charlotte, you keep that up and I'm going to come."

I look up at him and smirk. "That's the idea, sweetheart." I keep going, squeezing his cock and sucking hard. He bucks beneath me, and I go faster, meeting the motion of his hips as they rise.

"Charlotte," he warns, reaching to pull me off him.

I stay, and he releases into my mouth with a roar, his cock throbbing with his climax. I fucking love every second of it. Love having this man at my absolute mercy, his balls in my hand as he yells through his orgasm above me.

When he's finished, his hands fall away from me and he exhales roughly. His eyes meet mine. "That's it. We're getting married."

I laugh. "Look at us—who's surprised that we're both good at oral?"

He chuckles. "Two former law students who have to get in front of juries and judges constantly, good at oral? Crazy."

I crawl up beside him, fully intent on relaxing, but he turns and pulls me beneath him, capturing my mouth with his. His kisses are drugging, sensual experiences that I've never had before. I thread our legs together as he gently thrusts against me, our bodies leaving no space between us. For as large as he is, we absolutely fit together. Something I wouldn't have anticipated.

"Did you bring condoms?" he asks.

I laugh. "Are you kidding? Of course I did."

"I did, too. I just wanted to see if you were as prepared as I was."

"Are you going to grab them?"

He rolls off me in response, and I watch as he digs through his bag and produces a handful. "Think this will do?"

I shrug. "I've got backup if not. Plus, you should look in that drawer."

He raises a brow, then promptly inspects the bedside table. "Wow," he drawls. "They really, *really* were prepared."

My answering laugh dies as he climbs back onto the bed and resettles between my legs, his cock already at half-mast. I'm tempted to ask him how the hell this is going to work—*if* this is going to work—when we get out of this bubble, but decide I'd rather spend the time getting thoroughly fucked.

Literally, not figuratively.

He slides down my body, trailing hot, wet kisses as he goes. His hands caress in one moment, grab and squeeze another, mapping me as though he's an explorer in a new world. His eyes, when they meet mine, are just as hungry as they were at the beginning of this, hooded and blown with lust and wonder. I'm addicted to it.

He spreads my legs and settles in again, his mouth stoking me to near-bliss. He's got me on the edge in under a minute, and I reach for his hair. The dark auburn strands are silky and thick, pretty much exactly like the rest of him, and I gasp when he pushes a meaty finger inside me.

"Oh, God." My voice is low, animalistic.

He pushes another finger in and works me, sucking my clit exactly how I need it. I don't know how he's figured out the way to play my body already and I don't care. I shouldn't be surprised he's a studious man, not really.

"You want more, sweet girl?"

"Please," I gasp, uncaring that he's got me begging.

He rises and grabs a condom, rolling it on and returning as quickly as possible. He braces himself above me, looking down with an expression that borders on reverence. "You sure about this?"

"Levi, if you don't get your cock in me within seconds—"

He pushes into me, and we both groan. His lips meet mine as he pulls out, then pushes farther in. It takes another few times before he's fully in me, and he stills, letting the both of us adjust. I've never felt more full in my life.

"You're so fucking tight," he says against my neck.

I grab his hair and pull him up to look him in the eyes. "That's because you're huge, Levi. Now shut up and show me what you've got."

His eyes darken. "Yes, ma'am."

He pulls out and pushes in again, his hips swiveling deliciously as he kisses me deeply. I'm surrounded by him, his beautiful body hovering above me, his forehead on mine, his ocean eyes never leaving mine as he watches intently, looking for my reaction to every angle, every thrust, every swirl of his hips.

It's hot as hell.

I give him what he wants, telling him exactly how I like it, whispering how good he feels, and relishing each second of his attention. He is easily the most skilled lover I've ever had, and even now, in the middle of it, I'm already mourning the potential loss of him.

"Pillow," I instruct.

He understands immediately, stopping to position a pillow beneath my hips and change the angle. When he enters me again, the bliss is undeniable. "Fuck, Charlotte."

Delicious heat begins to swirl, gathering and tightening as

Levi's rhythm increases. He angles himself up, raking his gaze over me, eyes flaring at the sight of my tits bouncing with every thrust he makes. "Don't stop," I pant.

"Never."

"I'm almost there."

His grin is filthy. "Oh, I know. I can feel the way you're tightening on my cock, sweetheart. And when you come, it's going to be the best one you've ever had."

I can't summon the faux outrage over the egotistical statement, because it's absolutely true. My entire body is on fire, slick with sweat beneath him. He swivels his hips again, somehow going even deeper, then reaches between us to stroke my clit.

I detonate. My entire body shudders as white waves of rapture pour over me, and I hold onto Levi to keep myself tethered to the earth. I moan and writhe beneath him, pure instinct taking over to wring every last bit of pleasure out of the orgasm, as he murmurs praise above me. The moment is incandescent, bubbles of sensation floating from my hair follicles to my toes.

He doesn't stop moving. "Ready for more?"

My eyes snap open and meet his as I gasp for breath.

He smirks. "I'm not done with you. Not even close. Turn over. I want to see that glorious ass as I fuck you."

My limbs feel like jelly as he piles more pillows, then gets on his knees behind me. His hands skate down my back and around the globes of my ass.

"Way better than my fantasies, Charlotte." He positions himself and thrusts in, sending a riot of sensation through me. "My God. So. Much. Better." He punctuates each word with his cock.

I turn just enough so that I can see him, and the sight is enough to send me careening towards another orgasm. His *body*. All thick, taut muscle, his inked arms bracketing my hips as he pistons into me, his brow furrowed in concentration, sweat dripping down his forehead.

He is carnal debauchery at its finest, and I am ruined.

I will never be the same again.

I lose all sense of time, knowing only the sensation of his glorious cock pounding into me, hitting a pleasure spot I didn't know existed, his fingers once again reaching around to play with my clit. He loses his rhythm, then finds it again, going faster, faster, until he pushes into me so hard it almost hurts, and stills.

"Fuck, Charlotte!" He comes, falling onto my back as he groans, his hips canting upward as his massive cock throbs inside me.

I reach up and behind me, finding his hair and stroking it. He exhales, his breath on my neck, before he grabs us and rolls us off the pillows, keeping us connected even as we lay on our sides. His lips trail kisses along my shoulder, and maybe it *is* the orgasms talking, but I could absolutely get used to this.

"Do you want kids?"

The question takes me by surprise. "You're still inside me, wrapped in a condom, and you're asking me now?"

His lips meet my shoulder again, staying against the skin as he answers. "I do. I want a ton of the little rug rats, as many as possible."

"This requires face to face, Levi."

He consents, huffing a gentle command of, "Don't you dare get under those covers" as he pulls out. He disposes of the condom while I set the bed back to rights, then climbs back onto the bed. He props himself against the pillows, naked and without a care, and I do the same.

"You might be the most gorgeous creature I have ever seen," he murmurs, his gaze roaming appreciatively over my body. "You should know that I'd prefer you naked and wrapped in my arms constantly."

I snort. "Okay."

His eyes flare and he moves closer, grabbing onto my hip and stroking around to my ass. "Charlotte. You are sexy as hell. Especially now, after you've been thoroughly fucked."

He's dead serious, and something about the earnestness in his eyes thaws a part of me I didn't even know had hardened. "Thank you," I answer softly. "And, yes. Kids sound amazing. Terrifying and overwhelming, but amazing."

His face lights up. "Yeah?"

I grin. "Yeah."

CHAPTER 11

LEVI

EVENTUALLY, WE PUT our clothes back on and leave the bedroom. I'd like the record to show that I had little interest in going back out to the rest of the house, but Charlotte pointed out that the contract had actually included a minimum amount of time that we have to spent in front of cameras.

Fortified with a snack and glasses of water—neither of us are interested in drinking anything besides that—we settle once more on opposite ends of the couch with her feet in my lap.

"Tell me something," she begins. "And I know the cameras are on and you may not want to answer this, but I'm not judging you."

"Anyone who begins their opening statement with words about not judging someone is absolutely judging, Char." My muscles tense. That sex may have been the most incredible sex of my life, but I have a feeling I know exactly what she's going to ask. And no amount of sex is going to make this any easier.

"When we graduated, you had the opportunity to work for any firm you wanted. Why did you pick the one you did? You had to know who their clients were."

I sigh. "I knew that's what you were going to ask."

Those hazel eyes of hers, the ones that always see so much, don't hold back now. But her voice is soft. "Help me understand, Levi. Because…" She bites her lip. "Do you believe in what you're doing?"

Bullseye. I shift on the couch, bringing my leg up and bending it against the cushions so I can look directly at her. There's so much I want to say, so much I *need* to say, and over the span of a precious few hours, Charlotte Kelly has become the exact woman I want to give these words to. Because I think she's the one—the only one—who can offer me the salvation I so desperately need.

And make no mistake: I am in need of saving.

"Every time I lost to you, I went home and got so drunk I couldn't function the next day," I tell her. "And I was drinking to your success. Congratulating you and your clients on a job well fucking done. It was a *relief* to lose those cases to you."

"Levi." The uncharacteristic understanding in her voice is nearly too much.

I keep going. "I took the job because it paid the most. It was that simple. I wasn't interested in making friends, or a work-life balance, or anything other than making money. I wanted a firm that would reward me for being relentless. Ruthless. Willing to go the distance and then some. I proved myself in three years. By the time I was a fourth-year associate, I was second-chairing the biggest cases the firm had. By the time I was a sixth year, the firm's biggest client wanted me to be their attorney and not the guy who'd trained me. They fired him off their cases and demanded my firm make me a partner."

"Damn." Her eyebrows rise. "Impressive."

I shrug. "I was good. I *am* good. You know that."

"Ah, to have the ego and privilege of a straight white guy," she chuckles. "But keep going."

"Once I became a partner, I was untouchable. Funny how that

happens when you control the firm's relationship with a half-billion-dollar client."

She whistles low. "You don't sound happy."

I meet her eyes. "That's because I'm not."

"Then *why*, Levi?"

"Because I never wanted to feel the way I felt when we were kids. I still don't. I saw what my parents sacrificed—and Charlotte, we weren't even poverty level. There were people in that trailer park who were much, *much* worse off than us. But it didn't matter, because I saw what it did to them. The stress. The constant worry. We were always one football injury away from financial ruin. Who knows how many times my parents chose to feed us over paying the bills? We went whole weeks in the summer with no electricity, when my parents made it seem like an adventure. But we knew. Of course we knew."

She regards me. To her credit, it's abundantly clear that she really isn't judging me. Not even remotely. Still, I feel like a law school textbook beneath her studious gaze, and it's unnerving. Eventually, she speaks. "And now?"

I exhale. "It's no wonder you're so good at what you do."

Her answering smile is so damn beautiful.

"Now…I don't know."

She tilts her head. "Bullshit."

I huff a laugh. "You're more relentless than me."

"Answer the question."

With a meaningful glance at the ceiling camera, I repeat myself. "I don't know."

She nods. "Next question."

"Remember how I said this wasn't a deposition?" I chuckle.

"That was before you gave me two orgasms," she says.

"Relentless," I repeat, raising an eyebrow at her.

"You said you had a twin and an older brother. Are they still in your hometown?"

"Them and my parents, yes."

After a moment, she grins with satisfaction. "You bought your parents a house, didn't you?"

My cheeks heat.

"Levi Hall, you're a fucking teddy bear and *no one knows*." She wiggles in delight.

"It's small!" I protest. "They wouldn't take anything other than a one bedroom. But it *is* on the beach," I note with satisfaction.

"Does your dad still teach?"

I nod proudly. "He does. He's won awards for it, too."

"Brothers?"

"My twin is the police chief. My older brother runs a bar and arcade. What about you?"

"Little sister is a baby lawyer at a firm back home in New Orleans. Dad lives with me." She purses her lips. "He hates it."

"Doesn't like living in the big city?"

"Doesn't like living in the *cold*, is more like it. But he can't live alone, and I didn't want him to be a burden on my little sister. Not when she's getting started, you know?"

"You're amazing."

She scoffs. "Hardly. Controlling, a perfectionist, champion grudge-holder...*those* I most definitely am."

"You say those like they're a bad thing."

"Aren't they?"

"Charlotte. Look at me. I represent the scourge of society. When I win, the planet literally loses. People's lives are worse for it."

"You can choose differently."

I cock an eyebrow. "I know."

"So why don't you?"

"It's not that easy."

"Yes it is, and you know it."

"Is this how it would be—you and I?"

She blinks, thrown off. "Shit. You went there. Again."

"I'm never afraid of the truth, Charlotte."

"And it's hot as hell." Her full lips tilt into a sexy smile. "Also: yes."

"Good." I move, crawling over the couch cushions that separate us to leverage myself above her. She spreads her legs in answer, and I sink down.

"Mmm, giving the cameras what they want?" she murmurs as I nuzzle her neck.

"Taking what *I* want," I answer, then raise up to meet her eyes. "Did you mean it?"

"Which part?"

"The part where you agreed to my inference that we'd...be something after this."

This close, I can see the gold flecks in her hazel eyes. Eyes that are absolutely going to be my undoing. They soften now. "I meant it."

Relief courses through me.

She strokes my beard. "But you should know that I'm looking into setting up my own firm. Closer to home."

I take the information in, and a window opens in the recesses of my mind. "Question."

"Mmm?"

"Have you ever visited Lucky?"

Chapter 12

LEVI

HOURS PASS. WE talk, we eat dinner, we talk more. We plan. We play games, and I win them all.

She hates losing.

I can't wait till she takes it out on me.

After a particularly brutal game of Chutes & Ladders—because yes, that was one of the games in the bookshelf—I put the lid on the game and stand, holding my hand out.

She takes it, rising from the table.

Wordlessly, I lead her to the bedroom. I've had enough talking. I know where my heart lies, and I know where hers does, too. We have a plan, and it's a good one.

Terrifying, but good.

I take us to the bathroom and turn the shower on. When I turn, she's already undressing, pulling her top off and revealing the flimsy lace bralette that serves only to make my mouth water. Moving quickly, I remove my shirt and shuck my sweatpants and briefs, my eyes never leaving Charlotte's body.

She pulls the bralette off, then her leggings and panties, her own gaze roaming my body in return.

She's fucking flawless. A goddess in human form sent to offer me forgiveness, her thick caramel-colored hair hanging down to the tips of her dusky rose nipples, her hips and belly round and inviting, her pussy bare. I nearly sink to my knees right there to worship her, but pull the curtain to the side and gesture instead.

It's a tight fit. My head hits the top of the shower head, and there won't be a second where we're not touching each other. Her grin bright, she tips her head into the water and wets her hair, rivulets of water running down her breasts. My cock thickens. I reach for the pouf and body wash I'd made sure were in here earlier, then work up a lather. When she opens her eyes, I meet them. "Let me wash you."

Her pupils flare as I get to work, taking my time and making sure to get every inch of her body. When I finish, she returns the favor, then I wash her hair, soaping the long, silky strands and massaging her head before she rinses. Again, she does the same for me, scraping her nails into my scalp and nearly sending me into a meditative state while doing it.

Grabbing the shower head, I disconnect it and bring her back to my front, making sure she's warm.

"What are you doing?" she murmurs.

In answer, I adjust the water, finding the setting that sends concentrated jets out of the shower head, and guiding it down her belly. She sucks in a breath when I get to her pussy. "Making you come."

I aim the water at her clit, and she reacts instantly, gasping as her body tenses against mine. "Too much?"

She shakes her head. "Move it around and pull it away some."

I obey, cupping a heavy breast in my other hand as I do so. Her legs quiver, and I bend my knees to take her weight. "Lean back," I say in her ear. "I've got you."

Her hand moves to grab the back of my neck. "There," she pants, slamming her free hand against the tile for balance. "Right there."

I do exactly as she instructs and her fingers dig into my neck.

A flush blooms across her chest as she nears her climax, and then, with a deep moan, she comes. I move the water away the second her legs shift, turning it back to its original setting and moving it over her to keep her warm.

After I replace it and she's in my arms, the stream hitting my back, she blinks hazy eyes up at me. "How did you know?"

"Know what?"

"That when I was first in here, I fantasized about you making me come with that shower head."

I chuckle. "I didn't." Then I slant my mouth over hers, kissing her deeply, relishing her taste.

Eventually, we get out and dry off, and I plug in the dryer for her hair. "For the record," she states, arching her eyebrows in the mirror, "I would never wash my hair at night. And I certainly wouldn't be drying it without a multitude of products and the right brush."

I pull her to me and kiss her shoulder, holding her gaze in our reflection. "Will you let me do it?"

"You want to dry my hair?" she clarifies.

"I want to do anything you'll let me do." Then I turn the dryer on.

I study her while I work, getting a closer look at the splash of freckles across her shoulders, the dimples above her ass, the way she shivers when I touch a certain part of her shoulder. My own hair has air-dried by the time I finish and roll the cord around the dryer, and I let her take me out of the bathroom and into the bedroom without a word.

She backs me onto the bed, sitting me down on the edge and grabbing a pillow to toss on the ground, then sinking to her knees before me. My cock jumps to life as her hair falls around her shoulders, the image already searing itself into a core memory that I absolutely will never forget, as long as I live. "What I wouldn't give to tell law school Levi that this would happen in a decade," I confess, threading my fingers through her silky locks to push it back from her face. "You, on your knees in front of me. So fucking beautiful and perfect, Charlotte."

She tilts her head and grins naughtily. "I bet you say that to all the girls about to suck your cock."

I groan, letting my head fall back. "Shit. Keep talking like that and I won't last long at all."

Her tongue darts out, wetting her lips as she scrapes her nails up my legs and inner thighs. "How do you want to get off, Levi? Do you want to come in my mouth?"

I shake my head. God bless this woman, she'd already let me do that. "Let me fuck those beautiful tits of yours."

Her eyes flare, and I know I've hit the mark. She reaches for the lube in the drawer, but I take it from her with a smirk.

"I'll do it. Any excuse to get my hands on you, gorgeous."

She moves quickly, before I can react, taking my cock into her mouth and guiding it to hit the back of her throat. My hips jerk as I choke out another groan. "Fuucckkk," I rasp.

She hums around me, working me over with her exquisite mouth, bringing me to the edge in fucking seconds. "Charlotte," I warn.

Popping off with an audible smack, she grins up at me like she's been licking her favorite popsicle. "Don't tell me you don't want me to lick you." She rolls her tongue around my head. "To suck you." Her mouth opens, and she sucks me in.

Fuck me. She's edging me, and she fucking knows it. "Naughty girl," I manage, my whole world locking down on her and her alone.

She blinks up at me, all doe-eyed innocence even as she runs a fingernail beneath my balls.

I'm going to die. And I'm going to be the happiest mother fucker who ever died. *Here lies Levi Hall. Died of a woman's hot mouth.* Heat coils at the base of my spine and I'm pretty sure the words "holy fuck" and "please" leave me, along with a string of nonsense.

Right when I can't control anything anymore, when I'm seconds from coming, she pops off again.

I exhale roughly, trying to gain my composure and failing spectacularly. "Charlotte," I gasp.

"*Now* you can fuck my tits, Levi." She produces the lube once more, but all I can do is watch in rapt fascination as she rubs her hands together and then puts the lube between her breasts, slicking them up slowly, giving me the show I am desperate to watch the rest of my life.

"Scoot closer to the edge," she commands, and I do so. With a few more directions, my cock is nestled between her gorgeous breasts and my hips are thrusting, and I'm pretty sure I'm going to marry Charlotte Kelly.

"Fuck," I whisper. My eyes snap to hers. "I need to be inside you."

Her eyes bright, she answers. "All that work edging you, and now you want my pussy?"

This woman. God give me strength. I pull her to standing and crash my lips against hers as I turn us. "Bend over the bed, gorgeous."

When she's bent over, she arches her back and looks over her shoulder to wink at me. "Fill me up, Levi."

I roll on the condom and position myself behind her, nudging just enough to pull a moan out of her. The two of us are in perfect tune, our bodies moving together as though we've been together this entire decade. It's everything I've ever wanted.

She is everything I have ever wanted.

"This is going to be fast, sweetheart. But don't worry." I thrust into her, holding and letting her adjust. "If you don't come like this, I'll bury my tongue in you until you do."

"Fuck. Levi."

I pull out to the tip. "Tell me what you need."

She wiggles her plush ass. "Your dick, baby. Give it to me."

I bury myself to the hilt again. "Did you bring a toy?"

A deep chuckle emerges. "No. Didn't know how or if I'd use it if I did."

"Next time, then. Play with yourself. Get yourself there with me."

I know the instant she turns the corner. Her pussy tightens, the walls constricting around my cock like the best, most incredible vise on the planet. "That's it," I praise. "Need you to come."

"I…am," comes the answer.

We tip over the edge together, the ecstasy nearly blinding me with its intensity.

Afterward, I tuck Charlotte to me in the bed, her head over my heart, her leg thrown over mine. She traces the tattoos on my arm.

"These mean everything, don't they?"

I swallow. "Yes."

"Too personal for the cameras?"

"Yes."

"Will you tell me about them?"

It takes the rest of the night.

Chapter 13

Charlotte

I WAKE UP beside Levi, blinking in wonder. I never sleep through the night. Ever. Not since my mom was alive, and even then at the end, most nights found me checking on her at least once, despite my dad being beside her.

Next to me, Levi sleeps. A not-so-gentle giant, he's on his back, one arm thrown up over his head and the other angled towards my side of the bed, as if reaching for me.

My heart squeezes. The things he'd confessed last night were so intimate, so deeply personal and raw, that I nearly came to tears. He'd broken his own heart, and it took him years to see it. I think maybe I'd broken mine as well, but in a different way. I'd needed to take care of my family when Mom got sick—and I regretted nothing—but I lost a big part of myself in the process. A part that I'd only just begun to get back.

"We should get married."

I lift my gaze to Levi's, his ice blue eyes warm in the sunlight. "What did you just say?"

He shifts, rolling onto his side and propping his head in his hand, a lazy smile crossing his lips. "You heard me, Charlotte

Kelly. Not immediately. But we're not leaving this house without a way to guarantee I get to have you in my arms every day."

"And if I say no?"

He licks his lips, the bastard. I already got an eyeful of his morning erection. "Don't say no. Say 'not yet' if you want, but don't say no."

"I'll think about it."

Smirking, he says, "I'll bury my head between your thighs while you do."

He disappears beneath the covers, pushing my legs apart and spearing me with his tongue without preamble.

I gasp his name, gripping the sheets as he works me. In seconds, he pushes two thick fingers into me and sucks on my clit, and of course I'm going to marry him. I flip the covers off him and go onto my elbows, watching the way his shoulders dip and flex with the attention he's lavishing on me.

He makes me come with his mouth, then he makes me come with his cock. In the shower, he grins down at me. "You ready to put me out of my misery?"

I continue to soap his body, memorizing the pattern of freckles that span his chest and down his abs. He's a behemoth of a man, his shoulders spanning nearly the width of the shower without trouble, his auburn hair hitting the shower head even as he smiles down at me. He makes me feel cherished. Safe. Things I haven't felt in a long time.

"Okay."

He huffs, amused. "I ask you to marry me and you say *okay*?"

I arch a brow at him. "We're standing in a shower. What do you want me to say?"

"Say *yes*. Say you can't fucking wait to spend the rest of your life with me. Say we'll have babies. As many as possible. Say you believe in me. Say *yes*." His eyes gleam with sincerity, the blue I'd once classified as ice now a warm, intense aquamarine. The weight of his palms on my hips is its own promise.

"Well, when you put it that way. Yes."

His lips find mine, and we stay in the shower, kissing and murmuring and laughing, until the hot water runs out.

"IT'S *GOT* TO BE NINE O'CLOCK." LEVI CASTS A LOOK AT the sun through the windows. We've made breakfast and cleaned up from it, but the producers haven't shown up to the house yet.

"Maybe we're such early risers that it just *feels* like nine." But honestly. I'd like to leave. I pat the couch. "C'mere. Maybe they need cuddle content."

He flattens his mouth, but then he shrugs and joins me on the couch, his head in my lap. I run my hands through his loose curls and he closes his eyes, moaning happily.

A laugh bubbles out of me. "I can't believe this."

"You'll believe it when I put a big, fat diamond on that ring finger," he murmurs, his eyes closed.

"You're really going to do it, aren't you?"

Now his eyes open and find mine instantly. "Charlotte. Yes. I'm dead serious."

"But we don't love each other." I don't know why I'm picking at this. I should shut up.

He shifts, moving his considerable bulk into a seated position and pulling my hands into his. He's in a long-sleeved black henley, the sleeves pulled up to showcase his corded, tattooed forearms. "Don't we?"

"It's been twenty-four hours," I remind him.

"Thirteen years," he corrects gently. "Plenty of time for me to have grown to love you. And for you to—"

"Have cursed your name more times than I can count," I finish with a smile.

"There's a thin line between love and hate, Charlotte. So you can hate me out of this side." He leans forward, his soft beard scraping my skin as he kisses one side of my mouth. "And love me out of this one." He kisses the other. "As long as you give me all of you. I don't care." He cups the back of my head and kisses me tenderly.

How has this man gone from being the absolute bane of my existence to the person I can't imagine my future without, in twenty-four hours?

Turns out, it wasn't that hard. All it took was some vulnerable conversations and numerous orgasms.

I kiss him back.

Thoroughly.

Five minutes later, the front door opens, and the producers come in.

Chapter 14

Epilogue

"PLEASE REMIND ME again why we thought it was a good idea to move to south Louisiana in the middle of the summer?" Charlotte's face is splotched from the heat and tendrils of hair fall from a top knot to stick to her face. Her chest heaves as we push the couch into position, and a bead of sweat rolls down her neck and into her cleavage. She turns, glaring at me as if all of this is my fault. As if New Orleans wasn't where she yearned to return to.

She's never looked more beautiful.

And that diamond and emerald ring on her finger is a stunner, if I say so myself.

"Because you said, and I quote, 'If I have to spend another winter up here, Levi, I'll cut off your balls.' And I happen to love my balls." I wink, then duck the cushion she swings at me.

Her phone rings and she pulls it out of her back pocket, then smirks. "Saved by the bell."

I collapse onto the couch and chug a bottle of water. We could have easily paid someone to move us down here, but there was something so *right* about loading up our belongings into a rental truck and driving away from Manhattan together. I needed to feel the experience of leaving more than she did; it's why I flew my brothers up to spend a couple of days being tourists and then help us load up.

I quit my job after the show. It really was as simple as that, and I've slept through the night ever since. Were my clients happy about me leaving? Not at all. Was my firm happy to see me go? Eh. They didn't like the seven figure check they wrote me, but it was still less than the bonus I would have gotten at the end of the year, so ask me if I care.

"That was my sister, asking when she and Dad can come over. And I set the air conditioner to 'arctic.'" Charlotte drops onto the couch beside me and looks around. "How the hell did we pull this off?"

"How did we buy a move-in ready house in the Garden District?" I grin. "Someone owed me a favor."

She eyes me. "Do I want to know?"

I shrug. "I mean, it's not like it was the mob…but you probably still don't want to know."

The house is a perfect New Orleans specimen: old, probably haunted, richly painted, beautifully appointed with the latest updates, and exactly what my bride wanted. So she got it. It's as simple as that.

"There are a lot of rooms to fill with furniture," she remarks.

"Mmm."

"Just how deep *are* those pockets of yours, Counselor?"

"Whatever you want, it's yours."

"That sounds ridiculous. But also: okay." The delighted giggle that escapes her is light and airy. I want to hear it always.

Her dad moved in with her sister. He wasn't interested in sharing a house with "horny newlyweds," as he put it, and even though I think it kind of hurt Charlotte's feelings, everyone seems to be a lot happier with this arrangement, anyway. A trolley bell sounds as it lumbers by on the street outside, and I twist to plant a kiss on Charlotte's temple. "You gonna let me work on putting a baby in you now?"

She laughs. "You've been working on that for three months now."

"I'm motivated. Highly." I slide a hand into her shorts.

Arching into my touch, she murmurs, "What if it doesn't happen? Me getting pregnant?"

"Then it doesn't happen," I answer. "I love you and the life we're building. If it includes babies we make, then that's perfect. If it includes kids we adopt, then that's perfect, too. Or if we decide it's just us and the ghosts in this house, then that's good with me."

"You make it sound so simple."

"Not to be blithe or disrespectful about it, but sweetheart, it's exactly that simple. Besides, I might be the one with the problem, so really this is me being proactively selfish. Protecting my fragile male ego and all that." She laughs, and it turns to a deliciously low moan as my fingers slide lower. She's wet. "Now. Back to my original question."

She shifts, opening her legs wider to allow me access. "I forgot the question."

"Let me eat your pussy on our couch in our new home."

Her hand finds my neck as she pulls me into a kiss, her full lips soft, her nails scraping against my skin. "Yes, please."

And so, we make love. First on the couch, then on the kitchen counter. We order dinner, and then I have her for dessert. Twice.

ALSO BY VALERIE PEPPER

GUIDED TO LOVE

~Small town romcom with men in uniform~

The Mechanic's Guide to Getting the Boss's Daughter (series prequel novella)

The Widow's Guide to Second Chances (Book 1)

The Barista's Guide to The Perfect Steam (Book 2)

The Grump's Guide to Chaos (Book 3)

LUCKY IN LOVE

~Beach town romcom shenanigans~

Dining for Love (Book 1)

Dashing for Love (Book 2)

Late to Love (Book 3)

ATLANTA GRANITE

~Rugby romance~

Worth the Try (Book 1)

SACRED RIVER

~Small town…with witches!~

Love Potion No. 69 (Novella, Book 1)

Karaoke Chemistry (Book 2)

STANDALONE NOVELS

Lightning in A Bottle (Angsty rockstar road trip romance)

STANDALONE NOVELLAS

Naughty All The Way (November 2023)

To Have and To Scold in the *Holidays & Hook-Ups* anthology by The New Romance Cafe (June 2023 - limited edition)

About the Author

Valerie Pepper writes steamy small town and sports romance hot enough to fry an egg on. Naturally, she's an incurable optimist and a firm believer in happily ever afters, even if it takes more than one try. She's fascinated with the idea of a capsule wardrobe, but loves clothes and shoes far too much to make a real go of it. She's living out her own second-chance romance in Birmingham, Alabama, with her family (and maybe too many shoes).

Get a free short story at www.authorvaleriepepper.com and follow her @authorvaleriepepper on most social media.